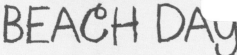

BEACH DAY

By Quinlan B. Lee
Illustrated by Steve Haefele

ISBN 0-439-81618-1

12   40   19/0

Designed by Michael Massen
Printed in the U.S.A.
First printing, May 2006

SCHOLASTIC INC.

| New York | Toronto | London | Auckland | Sydney |
| Mexico City | New Delhi | Hong Kong | Buenos Aires | |

It was a beautiful summer day.

"Wake up, Clifford!" Emily Elizabeth said. "We're going someplace fun today to meet Nina and Jorgé."

Someplace fun? Where could they be going? The dog park? The deli? The zoo? Clifford couldn't wait to find out.

While Emily Elizabeth and Clifford had breakfast, Mr. and Mrs. Howard packed the picnic basket and a big bag.

We must be going someplace far away, thought Clifford. But why was everyone dressed so funny?

Soon they were on their way out of the city.

"Mmm," Mrs. Howard said. "Doesn't the sea air smell wonderful?"

Emily Elizabeth held on to Clifford while he stuck his nose out the window.

It smelled salty and a little fishy outside. Maybe they were going to the deli.

Before long, they had arrived. Clifford couldn't see anything, but he heard a strange new sound.

It was a loud whoosh that kept stopping and starting, and starting and stopping.

What could it be? The wind? A train?

"We're here!" Emily Elizabeth cried.
We're where? Clifford wondered.
He started running to follow Emily Elizabeth, but something was wrong.
He wasn't getting anywhere. The ground was too soft.

Emily Elizabeth laughed and scooped him up.
"Need a hand?" she said.

The Howards set up an umbrella and chairs on the sand.
Mr. Howard picked up his book and smiled.
"Perfect." He sighed.

Perfect? But Clifford always thought the chair in the living room was the perfect place to read.

"Jorgé and Nina should be here soon," Emily Elizabeth said. "Let's build a sand castle while we wait. You can help me dig."

Digging! Now that was something Clifford *did* know about.

Suddenly, he felt something pinching his nose.
"Little Red, meet Big Red," Norville said. "You never know what you might dig up around here—maybe buried treasure."

Buried treasure? Like bones? Clifford wondered.

Clifford loved playing in the sand castle that Emily Elizabeth built.
When Jorgé came, he ran to show it to him.

But when they got to where it was, it had disappeared!

"Where did it go?" Clifford asked.

"A wave must have washed it away," Jorgé replied.

Just then, another wave came and tickled Clifford's toes. He looked down, but it was gone. Then a second later, it was back.

"Don't worry about the waves, Little Red," said Norville. "It's just water that likes to play games. It'll chase and tickle you. Some people even say it dances."

Dancing water? But there wasn't any music. Clifford was more confused than ever.

"Come on, let's go swimming!" Emily Elizabeth said.
She picked up Clifford and took him out into the waves.

He had a great time splashing and swimming with Jorgé and the girls.

Emily Elizabeth wrapped Clifford in a towel and snuggled him in her lap.
"Don't you just love the beach, Clifford?" she said.

So that was it! This was the beach! The waves, the sand, the smells, even the crab. He did love it!

But then again, anywhere Emily Elizabeth was, Clifford was sure to love.